P9-DXN-714

This book is dedicated to
preschool students everywhere

Text and illustrations copyright © 2007 Mo Willems

The images in this book are a melding of hand-drawn ink sketches and photography. The sketches were colored and shaded digitally; the photographs were taken in Park Slope, Brooklyn, and altered to expunge sundry urban debris and protect the innocent. The photographs are the author's (the Grand Army Plaza panorama required the additional skills and enthusiasm of Mr. Tom Drysdale).

All rights reserved. Published by Hyperion Books for Children, an imprint of Buena Vista Books, Inc. No part of this book may be reproduced or transmitted in any form or by any means, electronic or mechanical, including photocopying, recording, or by any information storage and retrieval system, without written permission from the publisher.
For information address Hyperion Books for Children,
77 West 66th Street, New York, New York 10023.

First Edition, September 2007
17 19 20 18 16
FAC-039745-22053

Printed in South Korea

This book is set in Typography of Coop/House Industries;
Century Gothic Pro/Monotype; and LTC Village No 2/Fontspring

Reinforced binding
ISBN-13: 978-1-4231-0299-1
ISBN-10: 1-4231-0299-1

Library of Congress Cataloging-in-Publication Data on file.
Visit www.hyperionbooksforchildren.com and www.pigeonpresents.com

KNUFFLE BUNNY TOO

A CASE OF MISTAKEN IDENTITY BY **Mo Willems**

HYPERION BOOKS FOR CHILDREN / NEW YORK

One morning, not so long ago,
Trixie took a walk with her daddy.

By now, Trixie really
knew how to talk.

959
Guess what I'm going to do. I'm going to show Amy, and then I'll show Meg, and...
T

And talk, and talk.

Trixie was excited because she was taking her one-of-a-kind Knuffle Bunny someplace very special . . .

school!

STAY B
B

Welcome
To Pre-K
Ms Greengro
My family went to
I went to

Trixie couldn't wait to show Knuffle Bunny to Ms. Greengrove and all her friends in Pre-K.

But just as her daddy
kissed her good-bye,
Trixie saw Sonja.

Manager
Dishwashers
THE CAT
ONE, TWO,
ONE PAIR!
Alphabet Bo
Books
MATH
Nancy T
Winter Books
ERIC CA

Suddenly, Trixie's one-of-a-kind Knuffle Bunny wasn't so one-of-a-kind anymore.

The morning did not go well.

Kuh-nuffle!

Nuffle!

Kuh-nuffle!

Nuffle

The afternoon was worse.

When the school bell rang, Ms. Greengrove returned the Knuffle Bunnies.

And the day got better.

Then, before she knew it,

it was time to go home

Trixie "ate" her dinner,

devoured her dessert,

brushed her teeth . . .

and tried to
escape the Mommy
and Daddy robots
from planet Snurp!

At half-past bedtime, Trixie was tucked in,

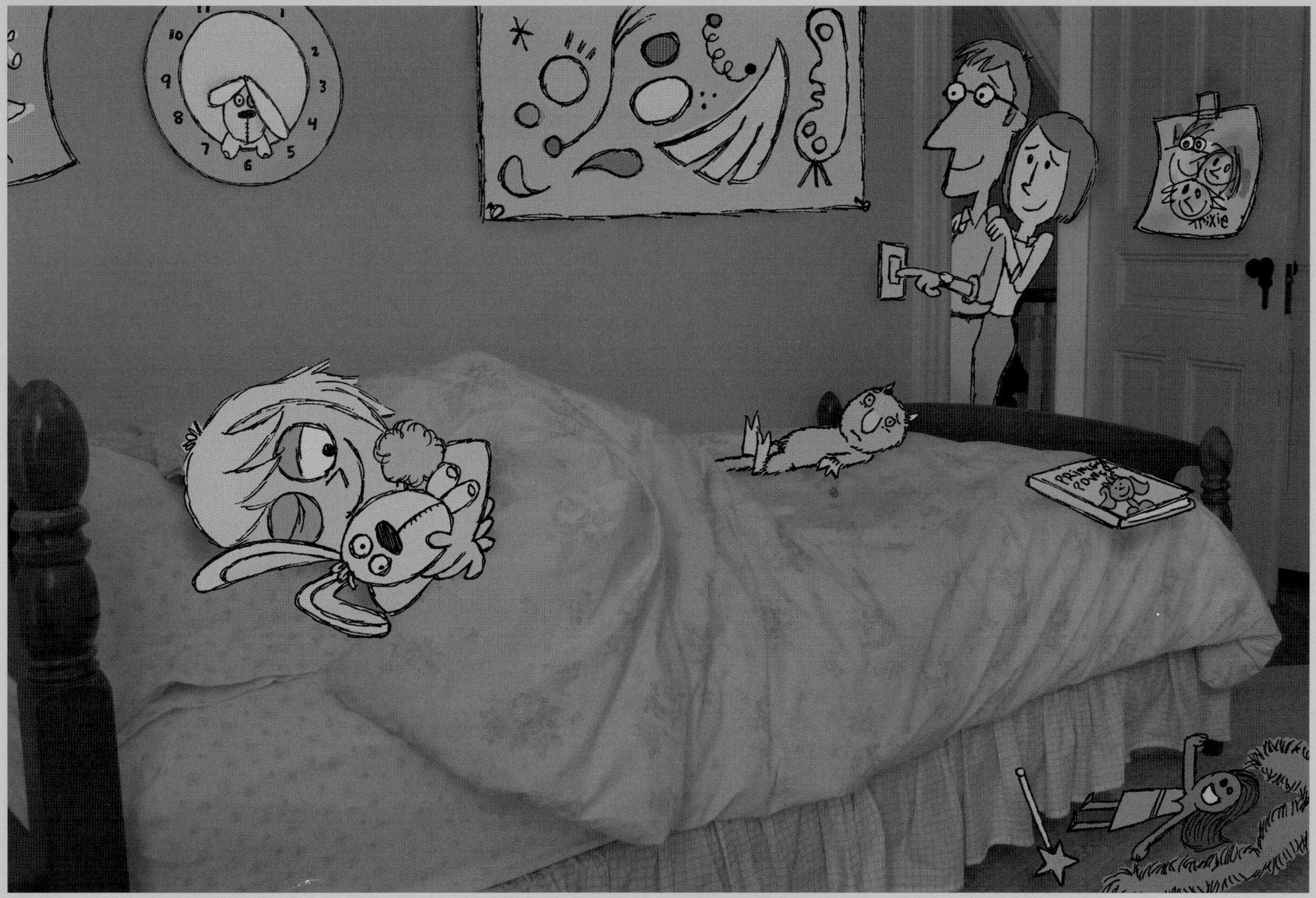

ready for sleep.

But a few hours later . . .

Trixie realized

something

Trixie marched into her mommy and daddy's room and said:

That is *not* my bunny.

Trixie's daddy tried to explain what "2:30 a.m." means.

He asked, "Can we deal with this in the morning?"

Trixie's daddy went to the phone.

Before he even made it
down the stairs,

the phone rang.

said a man's voice on the other end.

replied Trixie's daddy.

Arrangements were made.

959

Trixie and her daddy rushed across the neighborhood!

Trixie did not
want to be late.

Neither did Sonja.

There was an exchange.

And the Knuffle Bunnies were back

where they belonged.

said Sonja.

Trixie replied.

Then they both said,

at the exact

same

time!

And that is how Trixie found her first* best friend.

*Knuffle Bunny excepted, of course.

Special thanks to the real Trix and his mommy; Tom Drysdale; the Brooklyn Public Library; the Robinson family; the Lewine family; Ms. Theope; Ms. Holton; and the PS107 community.

EPILOGUE

The next morning, both Trixie and Sonja rushed to school.

The new best friends had a lot of catching up to do.

CONTRA COSTA COUNTY LIBRARY

31901068463282